W9-BAC-910

# HERCULES
## THE TWELVE LABORS

**A
GREEK
MYTH**

**THE EXCHANGE**

Should a hero
be loyal no
matter what?

# HERCULES
## THE TWELVE LABORS

A
GREEK
MYTH

## PAUL STORRIE • STEVE KURTH

HAMPTON-BROWN

*Hercules* by Paul Storrie, illustrated by Steve Kurth. Copyright © 2007 by Millbrook Press, a division of Lerner Publishing Group.
This edition is published by Hampton-Brown Company, Inc., by arrangement with Graphic Universe, an imprint of Lerner Publishing Group,
241 First Avenue North, Minneapolis, MN 55401 U. S. A.

On-Page Coach™ (introductions, questions, on-page glossaries), The Exchange,
back cover summary © Hampton-Brown.

Hampton-Brown
P.O. Box 223220
Carmel, California 93922
800-333-3510
www.hampton-brown.com

Printed in the United States of America

ISBN-13: 978-0-7362-3162-6
ISBN-10: 0-7362-3162-5

08 09 10 11 12 13 14 15 10 9 8 7 6 5 4

# TABLE OF CONTENTS

# INTRODUCTION

The people of ancient Greece believed that a large family of gods and goddesses ruled the earth. They lived on Mount Olympus and were known as the Olympians. While they looked like humans, the Olympians had special powers and abilities that humans did not. They were also immortal. This means they could never be sick or die. But despite their powers, the Greek gods and goddesses had human emotions. Stories about them describe their feelings of love, jealousy, or hate. Because the Olympians were so powerful, their strong emotions were dangerous to humans. They could cause great suffering when they were upset.

Greek mythology is a collection of stories, or myths, about the Olympians. Some myths tell about their contact with humans. The human heroes of the stories have great courage, strength, and intelligence. (Heroes usually had these qualities because one of their parents was a god or goddess.) Myths about heroes tell how they use their strength and intelligence to defeat enemies and overcome impossible **obstacles**.

Hercules was one of the most famous mythological heroes of ancient Greece. He was known for his amazing strength, courage, and **endurance**. Hercules was far more **muscular** than any other human on earth. His amazing strength allowed him to defeat almost

**Key Concepts**

**obstacle** *n.* something that stands in the way of achieving a goal

**endurance** *n.* ability to continue to do something, no matter how difficult it is

**muscular** *adj.* having large muscles

any enemy. He was so strong because his father was Zeus, the king of the gods. Hercules was also very clever. He used his intelligence to defeat his enemies when strength alone was not enough.

The legend of Hercules began when Zeus fell in love with a beautiful Greek woman named Alcmena. When Alcmena became pregnant, the king's wife Hera was furious. Hera tried to stop the baby from being born. But she was unsuccessful. When the child was born, he was named Hercules. This name means "glorious gift of Hera." It made the goddess even angrier. She swore she would make the child's life miserable. She got her **revenge**. Hercules suffered horribly his entire life. He endured a lifetime of pain and sadness. For his courage and suffering, he was brought to live on Mount Olympus when he died.

Myths about gods and heroes were part of the Greeks' oral storytelling tradition. Myths were also performed for entertainment. More stories were told about Hercules than any other hero in Greek mythology. These stories are still popular today. They are retold in movies, books, and plays. There are many different versions of Hercules's life story. There are also many stories about why he had to perform the twelve **labors**. This graphic novel tells one of those versions.

## Key Concepts

**revenge** *n.* punishment in return for insult or injury

**labors** *n.* tasks, chores

# MAP of HERCULES'S TWELVE LABORS

EUROPE

NORTH

THE
PILLARS
OF
HERCULES

1 NEMEA (Lion)

2 LERNEA (Hydra)

3 CERYNEA (Hind)

4 MOUNT ERYMANTHUS (Boar)

5 ELIS (Augean Stables)

6 LAKE STYMPHALIS (Birds)

7 CRETE (Cretan Bull)

8 THRACE (Diomedes' Horses)

9 LAND of the AMAZONS (Hippolyta's Belt) ✳

10 ERYTHEIA (Geryon's Cattle)

11 GARDEN of the HESPERIDES (Golden Apples) ✳

12 HADES (Cerberus The Three-headed Dog) ✳

✳ The locations of these legendary sites are
the best estimates of historians.

# THE LEGEND BEGINS

Long ago, in the far off land of Greece, there lived a hero named **HERCULES**. There has never been a man as strong, before or since.

His mother was **ALCMENA**, a **MORTAL**, but his father was **ZEUS**, the king of the **GODS**.

The **GODDESS HERA** was jealous that **ZEUS**, her husband, loved a **MORTAL** woman. Because of that, she hated **HERCULES**.

**HERO** great man; brave person

**MORTAL** human

**THE GODS** those who ruled the earth

**JEALOUS** angry

11

HERCULES WAS RAISED IN THE CITY OF *THEBES*, ALONG WITH HIS HALF BROTHER, *IPHICLES*.

EACH NIGHT, *ALCMENA* WOULD PUT HER SONS TO BED IN A GREAT *BRONZE SHIELD* THAT SERVED AS THEIR CRIB.

ONE NIGHT, HERA SENT TWO SERPENTS TO SLAY THE SLEEPING HERCULES, NOT CARING THAT HIS BROTHER WAS IN DANGER, TOO.

BUT *ZEUS* WATCHED OVER HIS SON AND SENT A *BRIGHT LIGHT* TO WAKE HIM.

EVEN AS A *CHILD*, HE WAS *STRONG* ENOUGH TO SAVE HIS BROTHER AND HIMSELF.

SON OF *ZEUS*, YOU MUST GO TO YOUR COUSIN, *KING EURYSTHEUS* OF *MYCENAE*, AND PUT YOURSELF IN HIS SERVICE.

THIS IS THE WILL OF THE GODS.

WHEN HE WAS A GROWN MAN, HE WENT TO THE *ORACLE AT DELPHI*, WHO GAVE MESSAGES FROM THE *GODS*, TO LEARN WHAT HE SHOULD DO WITH HIS GREAT GIFT OF *STRENGTH*.

THOUGH *HERCULES* COULD NOT SEE HER, IT WAS THE *GODDESS HERA* WHO SPOKE THROUGH THE *ORACLE* THAT DAY.

**SERPENTS TO SLAY** snakes to kill

**PUT YOURSELF IN HIS SERVICE** do what he asks

**WILL** wish, desire

# FANTASTIC CREATURES

THE JOURNEY TO **MYCENAE** WAS LONG, BUT **HERCULES** LOOKED FORWARD TO SEEING HIS COUSIN.

WHAT HE DID NOT KNOW WAS THAT KING EURYSTHEUS WAS **JEALOUS** OF HIS STRENGTH AND FAME.

SO, HERCULES, YOU SAY THE **GODS** SENT YOU TO SERVE ME?

WELL THEN, WE SHALL HAVE TO FIND LABORS EQUAL TO YOUR **AMAZING** STRENGTH.

THE KING DID NOT KNOW THAT THE QUIET WORDS THAT CAME TO HIM WERE WHISPERED BY JEALOUS **HERA**, HOPING TO DO HERCULES HARM.

YES ... YES.

IN NEMEA, BY THE **SACRED GROVE** OF ZEUS, A **FIERCE LION** IS MENACING THE COUNTRYSIDE.

I MUST WARN YOU, NO HUNTER OR HERO HAS BEEN ABLE TO KILL IT.

THE CREATURE'S SKIN RESISTS **EVERY** WEAPON.

**FAME** reputation, popularity

**LABORS EQUAL TO** tasks that challenge

**SACRED GROVE** holy group of trees

**MENACING THE COUNTRYSIDE** eating people

SIGNS OF HIS PREY evidence that the lion was near

YOUR HIDE IS AS TOUGH AS RUMORS SAY! You will be difficult to kill!

CLUB heavy stick; weapon

...STRIKE YOU DOWN!

PERHAPS NOT.

IF WEAPONS FAIL...

MY STRENGTH WILL HAVE TO BE ENOUGH!

**STRIKE YOU DOWN!**  kill you!

**FAIL**  do not work

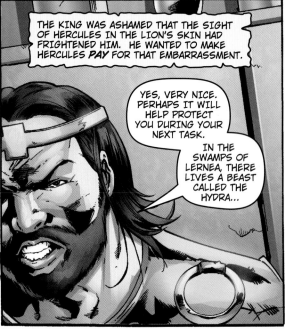

**HAS THERE BEEN NO WORD?** Have you heard from Hercules?

**DEVOURED** eaten

**MAKE HERCULES PAY** punish Hercules

BY CHARIOT in a wagon pulled by horses

IS POISON will kill anything it touches

ROUSE wake up

**THIS CANNOT BE!** Impossible!

THE GRIM BATTLE CONTINUED AS DAYLIGHT FADED. THEN, ONLY ONE HEAD REMAINED. THE IMMORTAL ONE.

WELL DONE! WE MAY WIN OUT AFTER ALL!

NOW, LET IT END!

AFTER HE STRUCK OFF THE IMMORTAL HEAD, HERCULES BURIED IT BENEATH A ROCK. THEN HE AND IOLAUS PREPARED TO RETURN TO MYCENAE.

IF THIS MONSTER'S BLOOD *IS* POISON, THESE ARROWS MAY PROVE USEFUL IN MY *OTHER* LABORS.

**WIN OUT** kill the monster

**GRIM** terrible, difficult

**STRUCK OFF** cut off

**PROVE USEFUL** help me

NO MATTER. It is not important.

MATCH MY PROWESS  test my skills

MONTHS LATER, HERCULES RETURNED.

EURYSTHEUS!

HERE IT IS!

HOW...? WHAT ABOUT...?

LONG MONTHS I TRACKED AND CHASED HER. SHE WAS FAST AND CLEVER. I THOUGHT I MIGHT NEVER CATCH HER.

FINALLY, I USED AN **ARROW** TO BRING HER DOWN.

THEN, AS I MADE MY WAY BACK, ARTEMIS APPEARED BEFORE ME!

SEEMS THIS GOLDEN-HORNED CREATURE IS A FAVORITE OF HERS.

SHE WAS ANGRY JUST **THINKING** THAT I HAD HURT IT.

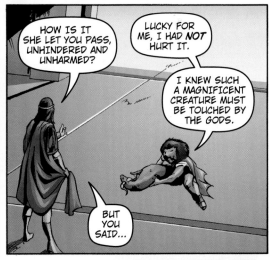

HOW IS IT SHE LET YOU PASS, UNHINDERED AND UNHARMED?

LUCKY FOR ME, I HAD **NOT** HURT IT.

I KNEW SUCH A MAGNIFICENT CREATURE MUST BE TOUCHED BY THE GODS.

BUT YOU SAID...

THAT I BROUGHT IT DOWN WITH AN ARROW. I SHOT BETWEEN ITS LEGS AND TRIPPED IT. THEN I CAUGHT IT BEFORE IT COULD RUN.

SINCE IT WAS NOT HURT, ARTEMIS LET ME FINISH MY TASK. I HAD TO PROMISE TO LET IT GO. NOW I HAVE!

**TRACKED** followed

**BRING HER DOWN** catch her

**UNHINDERED AND UNHARMED** without stopping you or hurting you

**TOUCHED** protected

LATER...

WHAT TROUBLES YOU, MY KING?

*Bah.* IT IS ONLY A MATTER OF TIME BEFORE HERCULES RETURNS FROM HIS *FOURTH LABOR.*

SLAYING THE ERYMANTHEAN BOAR WILL BE NO CHALLENGE TO HIM.

PERHAPS NOT, MY KING.

BUT THE FEARSOME BOAR HAS BEEN TERRORIZING THOSE WHO LIVE NEAR MOUNT ERYMANTHUS.

AT LEAST IT WILL NO LONGER HURT YOUR PEOPLE.

*TRUE.* I JUST WISH I COULD THINK OF SOME OTHER LABOR TO...

KING EURYSTHEUS!

HERCULES IS COMING!

IT IS AMAZING, MY KING.

HE CHASED THE BEAST UP AND DOWN THE MOUNTAINSIDE FOR DAYS.

FINALLY, HE DROVE IT INTO A SNOWBANK NEAR THE PEAK.

THEN HE WAITED UNTIL IT WAS EXHAUSTED FROM STRUGGLING TO GET FREE!

*EXHAUSTED?!?* THEN IT IS STILL *ALIVE?!?*

Y-YES, MY KING.

AND HE IS *BRINGING* IT *HERE?*

YES, MY KING.

*GO! RUN!* TELL HERCULES THAT FROM NOW ON HE SHOULD SHOW THE PROOF OF HIS LABORS TO THE GUARD CAPTAIN AT THE GATE.

*NOT TO ME,* YOU UNDERSTAND? *NOT TO ME!*

**DROVE IT INTO A SNOWBANK NEAR THE PEAK** trapped it in the snow near the top of the mountain

**PROOF OF HIS LABORS** evidence that he completed his tasks

**BEFORE YOU MOVE ON...**

1. **Viewing** Look at the illustrations of Hercules and Hera. What can you learn about them by how they are drawn?

2. **Conflict** Reread pages 11–12. Why does Hera hate Hercules? What does she do as a result?

**LOOK AHEAD** Read to page 29 to see if Hercules can finish a difficult cleaning job.

# GREAT CHALLENGES

**K**ING EURYSTHEUS WAS ASHAMED AT BEING SO FRIGHTENED ABOUT THE BOAR. HE BLAMED HERCULES AND WANTED TO EMBARRASS HIS COUSIN JUST AS MUCH.

FOR THE *FIFTH LABOR*, EURYSTHEUS SENT HERCULES TO CLEAN OUT THE STABLES OF KING AUGEAS IN A SINGLE DAY, A TASK AS IMPOSSIBLE AS IT WAS DISGUSTING.

THERE THEY ARE -- THE STABLES THAT YOU AGREED TO CLEAN!

*Ugh!* BY THE SMELL, I CAN TELL NO ONE HAS TOUCHED THEM IN *YEARS.*

I WILL DO IT, BUT YOU MUST GIVE ME ONE OF EVERY TEN ANIMALS IN RETURN.

*HA!* WHY NOT?

TELL ME, PHYLEUS, MY SON, DO YOU THINK HE'LL MANAGE IT?

I DON'T KNOW, FATHER.

**STABLES** horse barns

**TOUCHED** cleaned

**ONE OF EVERY TEN ANIMALS IN RETURN** horses if I finish the job

**MANAGE IT** be able to finish the job

23

EVEN WITH THE HUNDREDS OF ANIMALS OUT GRAZING IN THE FIELDS, HERCULES REALIZED THAT HE COULD NEVER *SHOVEL* OUT THE STABLES IN ONE DAY.

ROOM

HE HAD TO FIND ANOTHER WAY.

HE DECIDED TO LET THE TWO NEARBY RIVERS DO THE WORK FOR HIM.

THE TWO CHANNELS MET JUST OUTSIDE THE STABLE WALL.

POW!

RRRRUUMMMBBBLLLE

**GRAZING** eating grass

**SHOVEL OUT** clean

**CHANNELS** rivers

LEAPT jumped

MARVELOUS amazing

BLOCKED THE TRENCHES stopped the flow of water

DRAINED AWAY returned to the channels

ARE YOU INSANE?!?

I HAVE DONE WHAT I SAID I WOULD DO. TIME TO PAY UP!

NO, IT IS NOT!

I HAVE LEARNED THAT YOU DID THIS AT THE BIDDING OF KING EURYSTHEUS AND THAT THE GODS TOLD YOU TO SERVE HIM. YOU HAD NO RIGHT TO ASK FOR PAYMENT!

WHATEVER HIS REASON, YOU PROMISED HIM THE ANIMALS, FATHER...

WHAT? YOU TAKE HIS SIDE?

GET OUT OF MY KINGDOM, THE PAIR OF YOU! COUNT YOURSELVES LUCKY TO LEAVE WITH YOUR LIVES!

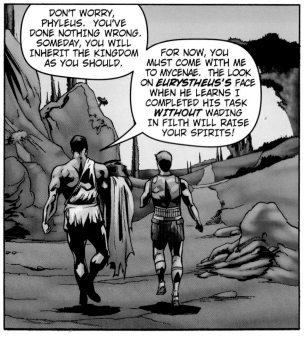

DON'T WORRY, PHYLEUS. YOU'VE DONE NOTHING WRONG. SOMEDAY, YOU WILL INHERIT THE KINGDOM AS YOU SHOULD.

FOR NOW, YOU MUST COME WITH ME TO MYCENAE. THE LOOK ON EURYSTHEUS'S FACE WHEN HE LEARNS I COMPLETED HIS TASK WITHOUT WADING IN FILTH WILL RAISE YOUR SPIRITS!

**TAKE HIS SIDE** agree with him

**COUNT YOURSELVES** You are

**RAISE YOUR SPIRITS** make you feel better

HERCULES WAS RIGHT ABOUT HIS COUSIN'S DISAPPOINTMENT. HE WAS NOT SURPRISED WHEN THE KING SENT HIM TO HIS *SIXTH LABOR* RIGHT AWAY, BUT HE WAS PUZZLED BY THE TASK.

KING EURYSTHEUS SENT HIM TO THE STYMPHALIAN LAKE TO CHASE AWAY SOME *BIRDS* THAT WERE BOTHERING THE FARMERS THERE. IT SEEMED TOO EASY.

WHEN HE ARRIVED, THE LAKESHORE LOOKED PEACEFUL.

HE DECIDED TO ASK ONE OF THE FARMERS MORE ABOUT THEIR PROBLEM.

I AM *HERCULES*. KING EURYSTHEUS HAS SENT ME TO DRIVE AWAY THE *BIRDS*.

QUICKLY! COME INSIDE.

WHY ARE YOUR ANIMALS IN HERE, INSTEAD OF THE PEN?

NOTHING IS SAFE OUTSIDE! THE BIRDS WOULD GET THEM.

THEY ARE MONSTERS! THEIR CLAWS AND BEAKS ARE MADE OF BRASS.

THEIR FEATHERS SHINE LIKE BRONZE AND DROP FROM THE SKY LIKE ARROWS!

WHAT THEY KILL, THEY DRAG AWAY TO EAT.

IT SEEMS EURYSTHEUS FORGOT TO TELL ME THE CREATURES WERE SO FIERCE.

NO MATTER. I WILL DRIVE THEM OFF.

NO! STAY!

FEAR NOT! YOUR WARNINGS SHOULD KEEP ME SAFE.

**THE PEN** behind a fence outside

**BRASS** metal

**FIERCE** dangerous

**DRIVE THEM OFF** make them leave

**ROUSE THEM** get their attention

KREEEE!

Thunk

Whhss

BECAUSE OF THE HYDRA'S BLOOD ON THE ARROWS, A SCRATCH WAS ENOUGH TO KILL.

Thump

Thump

HERCULES FIRED ARROW AFTER ARROW.

KREEE!

HIS ONLY FEAR WAS THAT HE WOULD NOT HAVE ENOUGH.

EVENTUALLY, THE LAST FEW BIRDS FLEW OFF. WHAT HAPPENED TO THEM, NO ONE KNOWS, BUT THEY NEVER RETURNED TO THE STYMPHALIAN LAKE AGAIN.

**FLEW OFF** left, fled

## BEFORE YOU MOVE ON...

1. **Character** Reread page 23. King Eurystheus wants to embarrass Hercules. What does this show about him?

2. **Summarize** Reread pages 24 and 29. How does Hercules use his intelligence?

**LOOK AHEAD** Why does Hercules begin to doubt the king? Read pages 30–41 to find out.

# EXTRAORDINARY PRIZES

FOR HIS **SEVENTH LABOR**, KING EURYSTHEUS SENT HERCULES TO THE ISLAND OF CRETE TO STEAL A MIRACULOUS WHITE BULL. IT HAD BEEN GIVEN TO KING MINOS, THE RULER THERE, BY THE SEA GOD POSEIDON.

MINOS WAS SUPPOSED TO SACRIFICE THE BULL, BUT IT WAS SO BEAUTIFUL THAT HE SACRIFICED ANOTHER BULL INSTEAD.

YOU LOOK UNHAPPY, HERCULES.

I DO NOT LIKE THE IDEA OF BECOMING A THIEF, CAPTAIN, BUT I HAVE NO CHOICE.

I MUST DO AS YOUR KING, EURYSTHEUS, COMMANDS.

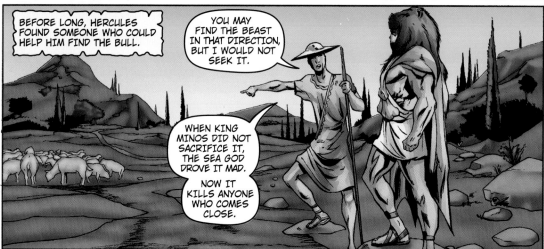

BEFORE LONG, HERCULES FOUND SOMEONE WHO COULD HELP HIM FIND THE BULL.

YOU MAY FIND THE BEAST IN THAT DIRECTION, BUT I WOULD NOT SEEK IT.

WHEN KING MINOS DID NOT SACRIFICE IT, THE SEA GOD DROVE IT MAD.

NOW IT KILLS ANYONE WHO COMES CLOSE.

ANOTHER DANGER THAT EURYSTHEUS DID NOT WARN ME ABOUT!

I AM BEGINNING TO THINK HE MAY NOT LIKE ME.

**SACRIFICE THE BULL** kill the bull for the gods

**SEEK** look for

**DROVE IT MAD** made it crazy

SOON, HERCULES FOUND THE BULL.

MRRRUUUH!

THEY STRUGGLED FOR HOURS.

FINALLY, THE CREATURE BEGAN TO TIRE.

WHAM!

THE BULL HIT THE GROUND SO HARD THAT IT WAS DAZED.

Ugh! THANK THE GODS I DO NOT HAVE TO FIGHT YOU ALL THE WAY BACK TO THE SHIP!

**TIRE** get tired

**DAZED** stunned; made unconscious

AFTER HERCULES DELIVERED THE WHITE BULL OF CRETE, KING EURYSTHEUS SENT HIM TO THRACE TO STEAL AWAY A PAIR OF PRIZE MARES OWNED BY KING DIOMEDES. HIS *EIGHTH LABOR* SOUNDED EASY ENOUGH, BUT HERCULES HAD LEARNED TO EXPECT UNPLEASANT SURPRISES.

GREETINGS, FRIEND!

ARE THESE THE STABLES OF KING DIOMEDES?

YES, THEY ARE. YOU MUST NOT BE FROM THRACE. ALL THE LOCALS STAY AWAY.

WHY IS THAT? I HEAR THE MARES THAT DRAW THE KING'S CHARIOT ARE AMAZING CREATURES.

SO YOU CAME TO SEE THEM?

INDEED I DID.

SORRY, BUT THAT WOULD NOT BE SAFE. TRUST ME, I AM THEIR TRAINER.

YOU SOUND UNHAPPY ABOUT IT.

THE KING LIKES THEM TRAINED AND FED A CERTAIN WAY. IT MAKES THEM DANGEROUS.

FOR EXAMPLE, MOST HORSES LIKE TO BE PETTED. THESE WOULD HAPPILY GNAW YOUR HAND OFF.

GOOD TO KNOW.

TO BE HONEST, I WAS SENT HERE TO STEAL THEM.

I DID NOT LIKE THE IDEA, BUT IT SOUNDS LIKE DIOMEDES IS NOT FIT TO OWN THEM. I HOPE YOU WILL NOT TRY TO STOP ME.

I DOUBT I COULD, EVEN IF I WANTED TO. GOOD LUCK TO YOU. THEY WILL BE BETTER OFF AWAY FROM HERE.

**PRIZE MARES** valuable horses

**LOCALS** people who live here

**GNAW** chew, bite

EVERY BIT AS NASTY  as mean

SETTLE DOWN.  Be calm.

GET NO TASTE OF  not bite

DEFEND protect

CRUEL mean

WHAT NOW? HERCULES HAS SUCCEEDED AT EVERY TASK I GAVE HIM. NOTHING HURTS HIM. NOTHING SHAMES HIM.

BUT WHAT...

YES! CALL FOR HERCULES!

FOR THE **NINTH LABOR**, KING EURYSTHEUS SENT HERCULES TO THE LAND OF THE AMAZONS. THE AMAZONS WERE A NATION OF FIERCE WARRIOR WOMEN WHO COULD FIGHT AS WELL AS ANY MAN. THE BRAVEST OF THEM, HIPPOLYTA, WAS THEIR QUEEN.

WHAT IS YOUR PURPOSE HERE?

I MUST SPEAK WITH HIPPOLYTA.

WHETHER YOU DO OR NOT WILL BE UP TO THE **QUEEN**.

I WILL BRING HER YOUR REQUEST.

UNTIL I RETURN, STAY ON YOUR SHIP.

IF YOU TRY TO COME ON LAND, MY COMRADES WILL STOP YOU.

**NATION** group, tribe

**WHAT IS YOUR PURPOSE HERE?** Why are you here?

**BRING HER YOUR REQUEST** ask her

**COMRADES** friends; fellow warriors

A SHORT TIME LATER, THE QUEEN ARRIVED.

HAIL, HIPPOLYTA, QUEEN OF THE AMAZONS!

HAIL, HERCULES, HERO OF THEBES. WHY HAVE YOU MADE THE LONG JOURNEY TO MY LAND?

BY THE GODS' WILL, I SERVE MY COUSIN, KING EURYSTHEUS OF MYCENAE.

HE HAS *COMMANDED* THAT I BRING HIM THE GOLDEN BELT YOU WEAR.

YOU PLAN TO *TAKE* IT FROM ME? DO YOU THINK I WILL NOT *FIGHT* TO KEEP IT?

IT WAS A GIFT FROM ARES, THE GOD OF WAR.

I HOPE TO *PERSUADE* YOU TO PART WITH IT. I RESPECT YOU AND YOUR WARRIORS.

I DO NOT WISH TO BE YOUR ENEMY.

HAD YOU TRIED TO *TAKE* IT, I WOULD NEVER HAVE GIVEN IT UP.

BECAUSE YOU *ASKED* AND BECAUSE OF THE RESPECT I HAVE FOR YOU AND YOUR ADVENTURES,

I WILL GIVE IT TO YOU AS A TOKEN OF FRIENDSHIP.

**HAIL** Greetings, Hello

**PERSUADE YOU TO PART WITH IT** ask you to give it to me

**TOKEN** sign, symbol

**HOSTAGE** as a prisoner

**SURRENDER** give away

**SET SAIL** leave on their ship; sail away

**TREACHERY** trouble

**MADNESS** battle

CATTLE cows

PASSAGE path to land

PILLARS columns; rock piles

LOOKOUT guard, watchman

WHEN HERCULES RETURNED, HE LOADED ALL THE CATTLE ONTO THE SHIP BY HIMSELF.

I DID NOT SEE HIM, BUT THE LOCALS TELL ME THIS GERYON IS SOME KIND OF MONSTER.

IT MAKES ME FEEL A LITTLE BETTER ABOUT TAKING HIS CATTLE FOR EURYSTHEUS.

RRRAAAAARRRR!!

YOU'VE TAKEN MY CATTLE!

I'LL KILL YOU ALL!!

GET MY BOW! NOW!

**LOADED** put, carried

**BOW** weapon

NoooOOOo!!!!

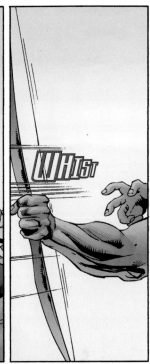

WHIST

ARrgGGHHH!

YOU KILLED HIM WITH A POISONED ARROW? I AM **SURPRISED**, HERCULES.

YOU ARE A MIGHTY WARRIOR. WHY NOT FIGHT IT FAIRLY?

I THOUGHT ABOUT IT. THEN IT OCCURRED TO ME THAT YOU, YOUR CREW, AND YOUR SHIP MIGHT GET SMASHED TO PIECES IN THE FIGHT.

oh.

**WHY NOT FIGHT IT FAIRLY?** Why not use your strength, instead?

**CREW** men, sailors

**SMASHED TO PIECES** hurt or destroyed

## BEFORE YOU MOVE ON...

1. **Character** Reread page 30. How does Hercules feel about the seventh labor? What does this tell you about him?

2. **Cause and Effect** Hippolyta gives Hercules her belt. What causes the fighting instead?

**LOOK AHEAD** How will Hercules get Hera's golden apples? Read pages 42–50 to find out.

# ABOVE AND BELOW

FOR THE *ELEVENTH LABOR*, KING EURYSTHEUS SENT HERCULES TO BRING HIM THE GOLDEN APPLES OF THE HESPERIDES, WHICH BELONGED TO HERA. THE GODDESS WHISPERED THE SUGGESTION TO THE KING BECAUSE SHE THOUGHT THE CHALLENGE WOULD BE IMPOSSIBLE.

FIRST, EVERYONE KNEW THAT THE HESPERIDES, THE FOUR NYMPHS WHO CARED FOR THE TREE OF GOLDEN APPLES AND THE GARDEN WHERE IT GREW, GUARDED IT CAREFULLY. SECOND, NO ONE KNEW EXACTLY WHERE THE GARDEN WAS.

BUT HERCULES KNEW THAT ATLAS, THE TITAN WHO HELD UP THE SKY, WAS RELATED TO THE NYMPHS. IF ANYONE WOULD KNOW HOW TO FIND THEM, IT WOULD BE ATLAS. SO HERCULES MADE THE LONG, DANGEROUS CLIMB TO ASK HIM.

*HA!* I CANNOT REMEMBER THE LAST TIME SOMEONE CAME TO VISIT ME HERE.

OF COURSE, MY HOME IS NOT TOO INVITING.

WHO ARE YOU? WHY HAVE YOU COME?

I AM HERCULES. I HAVE COME FOR YOUR HELP.

I WAS TOLD TO GET SOME OF THE GOLDEN APPLES THAT THE HESPERIDES WATCH OVER.

TELL ME WHERE TO FIND THEM.

**INVITING**  easy to reach; enjoyable

**WATCH OVER**  guard, protect

**OBSTACLE** problem, difficulty

**DRAGON** giant lizard that breathes fire

**A BARGAIN** a deal; an agreement

**EASE** move

EVERY HOUR THAT HE STRAINED TO HOLD THE SKY FELT LIKE A YEAR TO HERCULES. HE WAS GLAD TO SEE THE TITAN RETURN.

HERE THEY ARE! VERY PRETTY. EURYSTHEUS WILL LIKE THEM.

YES, I THINK SO, TOO. NOW, TAKE BACK THE SKY.

NO. NO, I THINK NOT. I HAVE HELD THE SKY FOR LONG ENOUGH. YOU CAN HOLD IT FROM NOW ON.

REMEMBER, I PROMISED TO BRING THE APPLES HERE. I NEVER SAID I WOULD TAKE BACK THE SKY.

WHAT?!?

DO NOT WORRY. I WILL TAKE THE APPLES TO EURYSTHEUS FOR YOU.

THANK YOU FOR THAT.

YOU HAVE BEEN HOLDING THE SKY MANY YEARS. I SUPPOSE IT IS ONLY FAIR THAT SOMEONE ELSE DO IT FOR A WHILE.

I WONDER IF YOU CAN DO ME A FAVOR, THOUGH?

CAN YOU TAKE BACK THE SKY FOR A TIME?

IF I FOLD MY CLOAK INTO A PAD FOR MY SHOULDERS I WOULD BE MORE COMFORTABLE.

HMMM. I SUPPOSE.

A PAD WOULD HAVE BEEN NICE ALL THOSE YEARS I WAS HOLDING THE SKY.

**STRAINED** struggled

**PAD** cushion

**FERRIES THE SOULS OF THE DEAD** carries the souls of the
dead by boat

**I SEEK PASSAGE TO THE REALM OF HADES.** I am trying to get
to Hades's world.

YOU ARE NOT DEAD.

NO, BUT I MUST GO.

JUST KNOW THAT NO ONE RETURNS FROM THE UNDERWORLD. NOT UNLESS HADES LETS HIM GO.

I KNOW.

THE MONSTROUS CERBERUS, GUARDIAN OF THE GATES OF THE UNDERWORLD, MADE SURE THAT NO ONE ESCAPED BACK INTO THE LAND OF THE LIVING.

AS HERCULES PASSED BY, HE KNEW HE MIGHT NEVER SEE THE WORLD ABOVE AGAIN.

ALONG TWISTING PATHS, HE MADE HIS WAY TO THE COURT OF HADES, LORD OF THE DEAD.

**COURT** home, palace

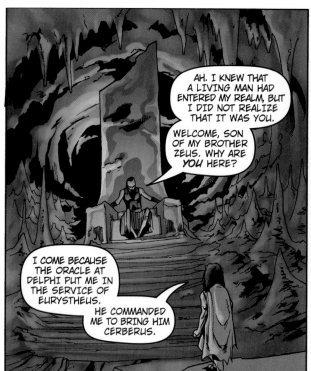

AH. I KNEW THAT A LIVING MAN HAD ENTERED MY REALM, BUT I DID NOT REALIZE THAT IT WAS YOU.

WELCOME, SON OF MY BROTHER ZEUS. WHY ARE *YOU* HERE?

I COME BECAUSE THE ORACLE AT DELPHI PUT ME IN THE SERVICE OF EURYSTHEUS.

HE COMMANDED ME TO BRING HIM CERBERUS.

DID HE? I THINK I SEE HERA'S HAND IN THIS. SHE NEVER LIKED YOU. SHE THINKS I WILL NOT LET YOU GO.

BECAUSE OF THAT, AND BECAUSE I DO NOT WANT TO ANGER ZEUS, I THINK I WILL LET YOU RETURN TO THE LAND OF THE LIVING.

THANK YOU, GREAT HADES.

WILL YOU LET ME COMPLETE MY TASK? CAN I TAKE CERBERUS WITH ME?

SINCE YOU ARE OBEYING THE ORACLE, I WILL ALLOW YOU TO TAKE CERBERUS...

BUT ONLY IF YOU CAN TAME HIM WITH YOUR BARE HANDS.

OH, AND TELL EURYSTHEUS THAT YOUR SERVICE IS AT AN END. TELL HIM I SAID SO.

GRRRRrRRRRr

**I THINK I SEE HERA'S HAND IN THIS.** Hera must have made him ask you.

**TAME HIM WITH YOUR BARE HANDS** catch him without using any weapons

AAIIᴇᴇEᴇᴇ!

NOW, RETURN TO YOUR MASTER.

I HAVE COMPLETED THE TWELFTH LABOR YOU GAVE ME.

NOW MY SERVICE TO YOU IS FINISHED.

THAT WAS THE END OF THE TWELVE LABORS OF HERCULES, BUT THAT WAS NOT THE END OF HIS ADVENTURES.

ALL HIS LIFE, HERCULES NEVER STOPPED MAKING DANGEROUS JOURNEYS AND FIGHTING AGAINST FEARSOME ENEMIES, BUT THOSE ARE STORIES FOR ANOTHER TIME.

**YOUR MASTER** Hades

**FEARSOME** dangerous

## BEFORE YOU MOVE ON...

1. **Sequence** Reread pages 44–45. Atlas refuses to take back the sky. What does Hercules do?

2. **Character's Motive** Reread page 48. Why does Hades help Hercules?

# GLOSSARY OF MYTHOLOGY TERMS

**AMAZONS:** a race of female warriors of Greek legend. Hippolyta is the queen of the Amazons. She is the daughter of Ares, the god of war.

**ARTEMIS:** the Greek goddess of the moon and of the hunt

**HADES:** the underground place where the dead live in Greek mythology

**HERA:** the immortal wife of Zeus

**NYMPHS:** in Greek mythology, goddesses of nature who are often represented as beautiful women living in the mountains, forests, trees, and water

**ORACLE:** a priestess of ancient Greece through whom a god or gods were believed to speak

**POSEIDON:** the Greek god of the sea

**TITANS:** according to Greek mythology, a race of giants that ruled the earth before their overthrow by the Greek gods

**ZEUS:** king of the gods, father of Hercules

# CREATING HERCULES: THE TWELVE LABORS

To create the story of Hercules's Twelve Labors, author Paul Storrie relied heavily on both Thomas Bulfinch's *The Age of Fable*, first published in 1859, and Edith Hamilton's *Mythology*, first published in 1942. Both of these drew their material from the work of ancient poets such as Ovid and Virgil. Artist Steve Kurth used numerous historical and traditional sources to give the art an authentic feel, from the classical Greek architecture to the clothing, weapons and armor worn by the characters. Together, the art and narrative text bring to life the mightiest hero of Greek myth, whose battles against gods and monsters earned him a place on Mt. Olympus, the home of the Greek gods.

# INDEX